Contents

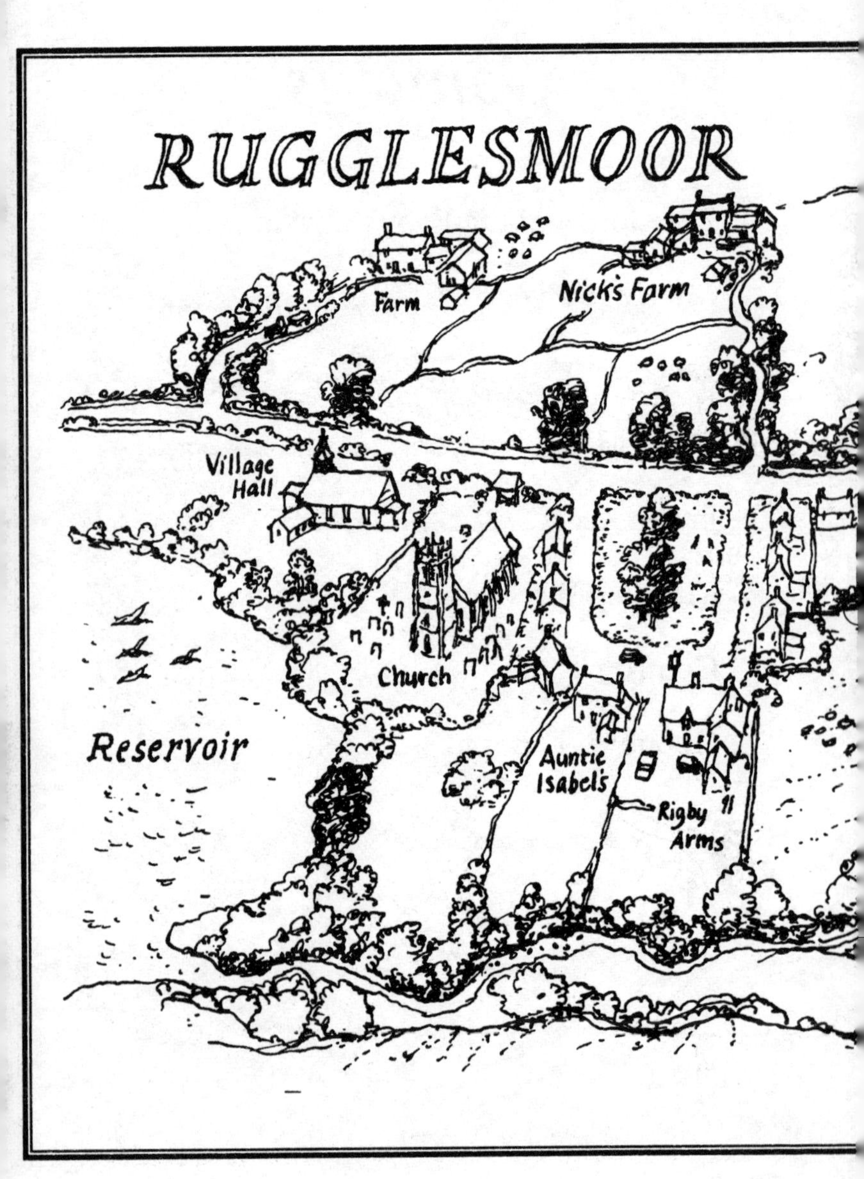

RUGGLESMOOR
Farm
Nick's Farm
Village Hall
Church
Reservoir
Auntie Isabel's
Rigby Arms

Strange happenings are afoot – above [illegible] ground – in this entertaining adventure story.

Alison Leonard has written a number of books for young people, including the novels *Tinker's Career* and *Kiss the Kremlin Goodbye*. She has also written plays for radio and the stage. She is married with two daughters and often goes on holiday to the Yorkshire Dales, the setting of this story.

THE MYSTERY OF THE RUGGLESMOOR DINOSAUR

ALISON LEONARD

Illustrations by

GARETH FLOYD

WALKER BOOKS
AND SUBSIDIARIES
LONDON • BOSTON • SYDNEY

To the children who write
at the Tattenhall Centre, Cheshire –
especially the Sandiway group.

First published 1993 by Walker Books Ltd
87 Vauxhall Walk, London SE11 5HJ

This edition published 1997

2 4 6 8 10 9 7 5 3

This book has been typeset in Plantin.

Printed in England by Clays Ltd, St Ives plc

British Library Cataloguing in Publication Data
A catalogue record for this book is
available from the British Library.

ISBN 0-7445-5480-2

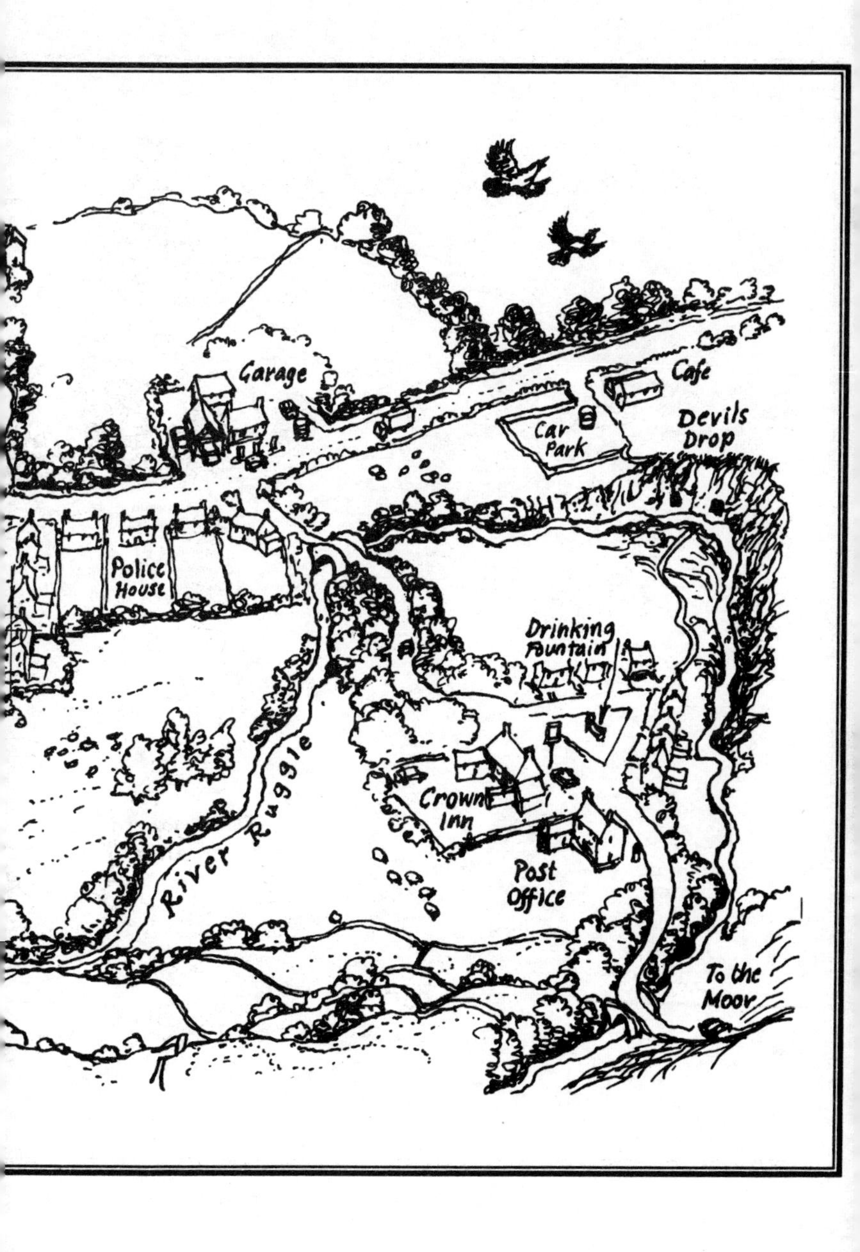
Garage
Cafe
Car Park
Devils Drop
Police House
Drinking Fountain
Crown Inn
Post Office
River Ruggle
To the Moor

Chapter 1

Boredom and the Baby

Danny and Lally were playing in the stream at the bottom of the garden when the telephone call came.

Lally was mad with Danny because he was splashing around like a fool instead of building their dam properly. Danny was mad with Lally because she kept bossing him about, even though he was ten and she was only eight.

"I'm the King of Rugglesmoor!" Danny shouted. "You are my servant and will do everything I say!"

But it was no good. Lally went on bossing. "Stop acting daft," she demanded, "and let me have that rock. That one there." She pointed.

"But I'm standing on it!" protested Danny.

"I don't care. I need it." Lally waded over and started to tug.

"Help!" shouted Danny, waving his arms about wildly. "Heeeeelp! Heeeee..." Suddenly he stopped.

Lally glanced up at him and stopped tugging.

Danny was looking at the bank. Lally looked too. Auntie Isabel was standing there.

"What is it?" asked Danny.

"Has it come?" asked Lally.

Auntie Isabel, her hands still white with flour, smiled at both of them. "Everything's fine," she said. "I was just putting the lentil pasties in the oven when the phone rang. It was your father. He was still at the hospital – he was so excited – he was in the corridor – you could hear all the hospital noises –"

Danny was holding his breath. He and Lally didn't dare look at each other.

Lally tried to stamp her foot and nearly fell into the water. "But what did he *say*?"

"It's a beautiful little girl," said Auntie Isabel. "Your mum's fine. They're both absolutely fine." Then she turned. "I left a trail of flour right across to the telephone..."

And she hurried away.

"Well," said Danny. "That's fine."

"Absolutely fine," said Lally.

"They'll be very happy," said Danny. He slid down off the rock.

Lally didn't have the heart to grab the rock she'd wanted so badly for their dam. "It's what they've always wanted. A proper baby. Not like us."

"Don't cry," said Danny.

"I'm not crying," said Lally. "I never cry." And, bursting into tears, she waded over to him, and they clutched each other till the stream splashed over their welly boots and soaked down to their socks.

The next day things were back to normal. They were arguing.

Danny was hunting for fossils in the gravel of Auntie Isabel's garden path, while Lally sorted her plastic dinosaurs into families.

"Stop that dinosaur squeaking!" ordered Danny.

"It's not squeaking, it's crying. It's a baby dinosaur, and babies always cry."

"Well, give it a piece of Auntie Isabel's chocolate fudge."

"Dinosaurs don't eat fudge."

"I wish we could have fudge for dinner," moaned Danny. "What'll we get tonight? Black-eyed beans and red peppers?"

Auntie Isabel was a cook. She made vegetarian food for the hotel next door, and Lally and Danny were getting the remains.

"I don't care about the food," said Lally. "I just want something to happen." She meant, something to take her mind off what was happening back home.

Danny and Lally had stayed at Rugglesmoor every year for three years. They liked being there and they liked Auntie Isabel, even though she was so scatty. They enjoyed the wild hills and the muddy lanes and the farm animals. They especially loved playing in the River Ruggle, rocky and swirling, that ran at the end of the garden.

Usually they came in the summer as a special treat, and often something exciting happened. Last year Danny had found a broken stone with a curly line inside, which Mr Brownlow, the policeman, said was a kind of fossil called an ammonite.

This time they'd had to come. All they'd done was wait for the phone call. And it wasn't even summer. It was April, cold and damp and misty, and they had to wear their sweaters and anoraks and welly boots every time they wanted to go out and play.

"I'm bored," said Danny. He hadn't found a single fossil in the gravel. "Where shall we go? Up the hill again?"

"May as well." Lally needed some more dinosaurs for her collection. Up the hill was the Post Office which doubled as a General Store. Danny often bought crisps there, and Lally got the kind of chewing-gum that gave you free plastic dinosaurs.

As they wandered along the lane towards the hill they saw Mrs Brownlow, the policeman's wife, hanging out washing on the line.

"Blowy! Dry these fair and quick!" she called. "Bored? Shame the Young Detectives isn't on."

Last summer Mr and Mrs Brownlow had set up the Young Detectives Club in the village hall. It was great. Mrs Brownlow had taught them invisible writing and Morse code and semaphore. Mr Brownlow knew about birds as well as policing, and he had taught them how to tell a lapwing from a curlew by its call.

Mrs Brownlow started to hang out her second basket of washing. "Has your little one arrived, then?" It wasn't fair. Everyone in Rugglesmoor seemed to know that Lally and Danny were waiting for their mum's new baby to arrive.

"They haven't phoned," said Lally.

"We ought to go," said Danny quickly. "Auntie Isabel needs some ... er –" he tugged at Lally – "some more lentils."

As they ran off, Mrs Brownlow called cheerfully after them, "You'll not get lentils up at the Post Office!"

"You lied," accused Danny in a puffed voice when they were half-way up the hill.

"They haven't phoned, today," retorted Lally. "They phoned yesterday."

Rugglesmoor village stood at the head of the valley. There was a circle of cottages round the village green, with the Rigby Arms Hotel next to Auntie Isabel's, and the police house a little further along.

An offshoot of the village crawled up the hill, where it had to cling on tight against the winds. Up there was a pub called the Crown Inn, and a little triangle of cottages, with the Post Office in the corner and an old fountain and drinking trough in the middle. The drinking trough had the inscription:

IF YOU WANT TO BE HEALTHY, WEALTHY
AND STOUT,

TAKE PLENTY OF COLD WATER INSIDE
AND OUT.

Danny wandered over to the garden wall of one of the cottages and started sifting through the pebbles that clustered beside it. Lally hopped round the fountain on one leg. "Healthy, wealthy and stou–out!" she sang, to the tune of "Here we go round the mulberry bush".

Danny rootled and rootled among the pebbles, but he couldn't see anything remotely interesting and was just beginning to think he'd give up. Then, suddenly, he gave a little shriek.

Lally stopped hopping, so abruptly that she fell over. When she got up again, rubbing her bruised knee, she looked open-mouthed at Danny.

He was standing face to face with a strange man. The man must have come out of the cottage, but he'd appeared as if by magic at the garden gate. Something about the way he stood made him look as if he'd been lurking.

He was short and square and had a thick square moustache. His face was covered in freckles, and he held a long thin hammer in his hand. The hammer had a strange kind of head, different from the kind that Dad used at home. The man wore thin plastic gloves, and ran the hammer loosely through his gloved fingers over and over again.

Danny and the man just stared at each other, not saying anything. Danny thought the grown-up should say something first. But this grown-up didn't seem to have anything to say.

"Oh!" said Danny, at last. "I was looking for fossils."

"Oh!" said the man.

"Well, I don't care," put in Lally, not sure what she didn't care about. "I'm going to the shop to see if they've got any dinosaurs hiding in the back."

At this, the strange man dropped his hammer. He glared at the two of them as if they were escaped convicts. Then he bent to pick up his hammer and quickly turned and disappeared back into the cottage as suddenly as he had come.

Chapter 2

Mr Hugo Byng

"Was he a ghost?" said Lally.

"Don't know," replied Danny. "Let's ask Miss Dora."

Miss Dora at the Post Office was a friend of theirs. She looked a hundred and five years old, though last year she'd told them she was only seventy-one. They didn't know what her surname was – everyone just called her Miss Dora.

"Two packets of chewing-gum and four if they've got dinosaurs, and what's that man with the hammer doing?" puffed Lally, as they ran in through the door.

"Lally!" said Danny. "Say, 'Good morning, Miss Dora!'"

Miss Dora got in first. "Good morning, Lally, good morning, Danny," she said. "And how's the family of dinosaurs this fine day?"

At any rate she didn't ask about the baby, thought Lally. "I need some grandparents," she said. "I've got some mothers and fathers, and I've got some children, so all I need now is some—"

"Talking of babies," interrupted Miss Dora, "any news about your little one?"

Lally made a noise as if she were about to explode. Danny took charge. "Miss Dora," he said, "there's a suspicious-looking man in the cottage opposite."

"That'll be Mr Hugo Byng. You should see that car of his!" Miss Dora dug among the sweet boxes to find the chewing-gum. "He's renting that there cottage while he goes hunting for dinosaurs."

"Have you got some, then?" demanded Lally.

"He's not looking for plastic dinosaurs, stupid," said Danny. "You mean real ones, don't you, Miss Dora? They're extinct! So why's he looking here?"

"He's got a rare old hunt going all round

Rugglesmoor," said Miss Dora. "Thinks the secret of the dinosaurs lies in this very valley, or some such tale. Never speaks so much as a word to no one. Cracked, he is. That's what I reckon. Cracked as a bell."

The door bell rattled and clanged, and Miss Dora said, "Oh!" Lally and Danny whizzed round.

Mr Hugo Byng stood, silhouetted darkly in the doorway. He still wore plastic gloves, and he was still slipping his strange hammer up and down in his gloved hands.

Miss Dora went back to her boxes. "I've got some under here, young lady, I'm certain of it…"

"She'll have some," Lally said to Mr Byng. "If anyone'll have dinosaurs, she will."

Mr Byng said nothing. His face seemed to tremble under its freckled skin.

"Ah!" Miss Dora pulled out three packets of chewing-gum with the lumps that showed they were the special offer. "Past their sell-by date. Have them free."

"Thanks a million!" said Lally, tearing open the packets. "Grandparents!" she breathed. "Look, Mr Byng! She says you like dinosaurs, too!"

Mr Byng turned up his freckled, square nose in disgust. He decided, at last, to speak.

"Anatomical features absolutely erroneous," he said. He spoke like an electronic announcement and dangled his hammer dangerously. "Modern education! One lightly-buttered cheese roll for my lunch, please, Miss Er…"

He doesn't even know Miss Dora's name, thought Danny. He must be cracked.

"Let's go to the Gorge," suggested Lally, next day.

Danny agreed. "I'll try in the stream for fossils."

They'd often been with Auntie Isabel to Devil's Drop Gorge. People had fenced off the best side so that you had to pay to get in. It was worth it – on that side the cliffs were steep and exciting, and there were caves at the bottom that you could explore with a torch if you borrowed special helmets.

You could get to the other side of the Gorge from the high part of Rugglesmoor village. It wasn't so exciting, but you didn't have to pay and it wasn't dangerous. You went along a tiny lane that led between the cottages from the triangle with the fountain, and tramped across a field. A stream meandered gently through the field before it ran down the slope to join the River Ruggle in the Gorge.

"What d'you reckon to him?" asked Danny.

"Who?" asked Lally. She'd already forgotten Mr Hugo Byng.

"Him! Byng-Byng! Thinks he's going to find dinosaurs in Rugglesmoor!"

The air was chilly up here, and high above them the lapwings were swooping and diving in search of places to nest. There'd been floods last spring, leaving little heaps of shale in the grass on either side of the stream. The two of them wandered across, with Danny stopping every so often to scrape through the shale-heaps with the toe of his welly boot.

About half-way across the field, he shoved the toe of his boot into a new pile of shale. His eye lighted on a stone just a little bit different from the rest. "Hey..." He bent down. "Look, Lally-oh!" Straightening up, he held out his hand.

The stone was small, and flatter than the ammonite he'd found last year. Lally leaned over and looked at it carefully. It didn't have tiny curly lines on it like the ammonite. It seemed to be half of a bigger stone that had been split open. On the split side was a distinct V-shaped mark.

"What is it, then?" she demanded. "Could just be a scratch."

"Could be," admitted Danny. "But I have a sort of feeling about it." He popped it in his pocket to think about later.

Lally found a big rock beside the stream, heaved herself up on it and laid out her new dinosaurs. Danny waded into the stream and picked about among likely-looking stones. But, having found one, they surely wouldn't find any more.

After a while, Lally got bored. "My dinosaurs are going to build a stone house," she said.

"Dinosaurs didn't have houses," argued Danny.

"Proper dinosaurs don't. But my dinosaurs are special." She hopped off the rock, crouched down and dipped her fingers in the stream. "Ouch! It's cold!"

"What d'you expect, bath water?" said Danny.

"Look, look!" Lally grabbed a stone and jumped up.

Danny was still gazing into the stream. "Have your hands gone all purple?"

"No! This stone! Danny, honestly, it's got marks on, like yours!"

Danny waded over. He didn't believe her.

"Where's the other one?" she demanded.

Reluctantly Danny handed her his stone. She took it and held it in her other palm.

"Wait a minute..." breathed Danny.

This stone looked split, too. And it had a mark on it. Not a V-shape, but a zigzag line.

Lally took the words out of Danny's mouth. "It's like something's toes."

"Footprint," said Danny. "A dinosaur's footprint."

Danny put his fossil back into his pocket, and Lally put the one she'd found into hers. They wiped their hands dry on their jeans and raced back to the village and down the hill.

Mr Brownlow was outside the police house, getting into his car. "Well, you kids," he said, holding a pipe in his mouth with his teeth. "What are my Young Detectives up to?"

"We've found something, Mr Brownlow," said Danny, puffed and proud. "Look at our stones."

"Detectives by name, detectives by nature, eh?" Mr Brownlow took his pipe out.

"Don't, Danny!" cried Lally. "They're our secret!"

"If it's stones you've got, it'll be just the thing," said Mr Brownlow. "Just the thing for Mr Byng."

"He's not going to have them! They're ours!"

The policeman frowned at Lally. "Withholding evidence, eh?"

Danny gave her an irritated shove. "Lally! What d'you mean, Mr Brownlow? This isn't like evidence for a crime, is it?"

"Not crime, Danny. History." Mr Brownlow leaned towards them. "Mr Hugo Byng, who's investigating in Rugglesmoor just now, is of the opinion he might be making the greatest discovery of all time. Right here."

"What discovery?"

"The last days of the dinosaurs. They don't know, you see. What was it that killed 'em all off? Was it starvation? Was it bitter cold? Was it an explosion from outer space? They've not an idea, one way or t'other. And Mr Hugo Byng is determined to be the one to find out."

"He's not having our stones," insisted Lally.

Mr Brownlow looked at her fair and square. "Laura, my girl, if you've got stones, then you might have got hold of some palaeontology stuff. Mr Byng needs all the palaeontology stuff he can find. It's your bounden duty to hand them over."

He patted each of them on the head and got into his car. Revving the engine, he wound down the window and leaned out. "Come on round when you've seen Mr Byng," he said, "and tell me what he has to say. Dinosaur Detectives, eh?"

"Lally, we've got to show people!" argued Danny, as they trudged on to Auntie Isabel's. "We might have the clue to the Great Dinosaur Mystery!"

"I don't care," said Lally. "Mr Brownlow called me Laura. And I don't like that Byng-Byng."

"It's nothing to do with like and don't like!

It's to do with history!"

"Well, I found mine, and I'm not letting them have it." Lally put her hands in her pockets. She counted her plastic dinosaurs in the left one and felt among the chewing-gum papers in the right. The precious stone was there.

"But can't you see it? TV camera crews, newspapers, all queuing up to speak to us: The Children Who Solved the Great Dinosaur Mystery!"

"Won't happen," said Lally. "Byng-Byng won't let us do anything. He'll want it all for himself."

Chapter 3

Celia

Parked outside Auntie Isabel's was a battered old green Citroën. Inside the house, Auntie Isabel was sitting down. That was unusual enough – but she was drinking coffee with a complete stranger. A young woman sat on the sofa, stretching her long legs towards the fire.

"Oh, Danny and Lally!" said Auntie Isabel. "We're just having coffee. Come and get yourselves warm. This lady was telling me some fascinating things – about stones and fossils and meteorites that may be lurking under Rugglesmoor..."

"Palaeontology stuff," said Danny, remembering what Mr Brownlow had said.

The stranger stood up. "Exactly!" She was so tall that Lally was afraid she'd bump her head on the beams in the ceiling. She had long bony arms and legs, and long blonde hair flowing down her shoulders. "Palaeontology! Let me introduce myself. I'm Celia Marchbanks, palaeontologist." She held out a long thin hand.

Danny took the hand and shook it. Lally hesitantly did the same.

"Ms Marchbanks is looking for fossils," said Auntie Isabel. "She says, if anyone finds anything, please take it to her without delay. It's desperately important, the question of how dinosaurs vanished away..."

"Call me Celia," said Ms Marchbanks. "And you are?"

"Danny," said Danny. "How do you do, Ms..."

"Celia," said Ms Marchbanks. "And?"

"This is Laura," said Auntie Isabel, "and she and Danny are staying with me while their mother is having a bab—"

"Lally," said Lally. "My real name's Laura, but I don't like it and everyone calls me Lally."

"Lally," said Celia. They all sat down.

"Now, Lally." Auntie Isabel's tone had changed. "I went out to post a letter – that was when I bumped into Celia, and we got talking. Lally, I saw Mrs Brownlow. And do you know what she said to me?"

"What, Auntie Isabel?"

Danny thought, Lally's completely forgotten she told Mrs Brownlow a lie about our baby. He burst out, "Ms March… I mean – we've found something. I mean, two things. They might be just what you—"

Lally stamped on his foot.

Auntie Isabel jumped up. "Lally, I'm ashamed of you! First you tell an outright lie to dear Mrs Brownlow and then for no reason at all you stamp on Danny's—"

"It's not for no reason!" Lally cried out. "It's our secret, they're our stones, and we needn't tell nobody –"

"Anybody," corrected Auntie Isabel.

"And if people don't stop going on about that baby I shan't let anyone see my dinosaur family ever again. I shan't tell them I've got three new ones from Miss Dora – in fact I shan't speak to any of you for the rest of my life!"

Auntie Isabel plonked herself back into her chair. She never knew what to do when Lally had a tantrum. Ms Celia Marchbanks drank her coffee in one gulp. Danny walked over to the log fire to warm his hands in a cross sort of way. Lally stood, defiant.

"I'm so sorry," said Celia Marchbanks. She twined her fingers together in a complicated pattern. "I seem to have upset things. Danny, Lally, I would certainly like to look at whatever exciting stones you've discovered. But I don't want to burst in on your secrets. I like secrets. I have some of my own."

"I don't know what's come over these two," said Auntie Isabel. "It must be something to do with this new—"

"Can we have a chocolate biscuit?" asked Danny.

"I must be on my way," said Celia. "But

Danny and Lally, I must ask you one small favour…" Her fingers untwined and twined themselves up again. "There is a man in Rugglesmoor at the moment who is, like me, aiming to discover the truth about the dinosaurs."

"Byng-Byng," said Lally, forgetting she'd vowed not to speak.

"Exactly! Hugo Byng! You've seen him?"

"Up the hill," said Danny. "Miss Dora at the Post Office says he's staying in a cottage there, and he thinks all sorts of exciting things might be buried under Rugglesmoor. If you're a dinosaur expert too, you must be a friend of his?"

"Friend of his – no." Celia looked anxious. "He and I used to work together, but we no longer do. We have entirely different approaches to our work."

"You used to be friends, now you're sworn enemies?" suggested Danny.

"Well, anyway," Lally broke in, "my fossil's mine, and I'm not giving it to anyone."

"Lally!" protested Auntie Isabel.

"Well, I'm not, and that's that."

And all the arguing in the world wouldn't shift her.

Upstairs that night Lally and Danny had an enormous row. Fortunately Auntie Isabel had popped round to the hotel to deliver her special aubergine bake and didn't hear them.

"Lally!" Danny shouted for the fifteenth time. "You heard! They might have starved, or got frozen in an Ice Age, or a meteorite might have come down from space with a massive explosion and wiped them all out! What if our fossils told them what actually happened?"

"I'm not giving it away!" Lally shouted back. "It's mine! It's magic and mysterious, I'm not giving it to anyone!"

"But you've got to trust someone, Lally." By now Danny was weary of shouting. He started to wheedle. "All right, Byng-Byng looks fairly revolting, but Celia doesn't like him. Surely she's OK?"

"'Call me Celia!'" mocked Lally. "She's just trying to worm her way in. 'Don't want to burst in on your secrets...' Give her the stones and she'd be off! She said so, nearly! 'The one that gets it,' she said, 'they'd be the most famous person in all the world...'"

"The whole palaeontological world." Danny had been practising "palae–ontological" inside his head and was pleased to get it all out in one. "But don't you see, Lally? It's not about who's first, it's about finding out. It'll change all the dinosaur books you've ever read! Those little cards with the chewing-gum, they'll say, 'For hundreds of years we didn't know how the dinosaurs became extinct, but now, owing to the Great Rugglesmoor Discovery, we understand it all!'"

"That's what you think," retorted Lally. "I've seen them, Byng-Byng and that Celia; I've seen the look in their eyes. They don't want it for chewing-gum eaters like me. They just want it for themselves."

Danny had run out of arguments. He

stomped over to the window and, sitting on the wooden window seat, he poked his head between the curtains and looked out over the village green. It was dark. Only the bright light from the Rigby Arms shone out over the grass. "So we're going to keep our precious stones in our pockets, are we? They'll be ours, and no one else's? What's the point in that?"

Lally came and squeezed in beside him. She poked her face through the curtains too. "I don't know," she said. "What shall we do?"

"We could throw them back in the stream."

"No!"

"Why not?" asked Danny. "It'd give Byng-Byng and Celia a fair chance to do the finding for themselves. It'd let us off having to decide."

Lally's mouth went down at the corners. "Wish we'd never found them. Wish we'd... Wish Mum'd never had a baby."

"Do you?" asked Danny. "Wish there wasn't a baby?"

"Don't know," said Lally. "I want Mum and Dad. I want to see them. I want them to come."

"Look at that!" exclaimed Danny suddenly.

A low-slung sports car, silvery and sleek in the moonlight, was drawing up on the far side of the village green.

"It's a – an Alfa Romeo!" breathed Danny.

A square, stocky man climbed out of the car and looked round. He took a torch out of one pocket and some sort of tool out of the other. Then he stepped carefully forward along the gravel. The torch beam shone out in front of him like a long pole, and he shifted the gravel on the path with his boot. Every so often, he would crouch down and scrape among the pebbles with his tool.

"Byng-Byng," whispered Lally.

"It's not a hammer he's got now," whispered Danny. "I think it's a trowel. Why are we whispering?"

Lally said loudly, "He's stupid. That gravel isn't from Rugglesmoor. It's from home –

from Leeds. It came in lorry-loads last summer, and there was 'Gravel From Leeds' written all over the lorries."

"Lally! You're fantastic!" Danny gave her a hug.

They were friends again. But they still hadn't decided what to do with their fossils.

Chapter 4

Devil's Drop

Next day, Auntie Isabel decided to take them to the exciting side of Devil's Drop Gorge.

"We'll say no more about yesterday's outburst, Lally," she said. "Celia had a word with me afterwards. She said that children are often upset when there's an addition to the family, especially when they're adopted. And do you know what Celia told me then?"

"What?" asked Lally.

But Danny said, "I don't think you should tell us Ms Marchbanks' secrets, Auntie Isabel."

"But..." protested Lally.

"No, Lally!" insisted Danny. "We shouldn't ask about her secrets! She didn't ask about ours."

Auntie Isabel looked put out. "It wasn't a *secret*, just an interesting piece of... What strange creatures children are. I'll never understand them if I live for a thousand years." She got into the car, and Danny and Lally climbed in the back.

Instead of turning right to the Crown Inn and the fountain and the Post Office, they turned left at the garage. Then came the sign:

DEVIL'S DROP GORGE
Beauty Spot
Caves
Terrifying Cliffs.

Danny whispered to Lally, "And last home of the dinosaurs!"

Lally screwed up her face and felt for the fossil among the chewing-gum papers in her pocket.

Auntie Isabel paid the money and they went through. Strong wire fences had notices on them, declaring: Steep chasm! Keep to the path!

Not many people were about, because it

was April and the start of the season. They wandered along, watching the occasional squirrel come blinking out into the sunshine. At the far end, some steps had been specially made to lead down to the river and the caves. Auntie Isabel had brought some biscuits, and they sat on a bench to eat them. Then they went down into the Gorge.

They had their helmets at the ready, and Danny carried the torch. No one else was going down the steep steps. Lally took Auntie Isabel's hand sometimes. Near the bottom she shouted, to get the echo: "Hello–o–o! Dinosaur, are you there–ere–ere?"

The children ran on ahead. At the mouth of the biggest cave they stopped. "Do it again," whispered Danny.

"Dinosaur–aur–aur!" called Lally. "Are you there–ere–ere?"

Out of the cave came the reply, "No–o–o!"

Danny turned to Lally. "It answered!"

"It said it wasn't there!"

Auntie Isabel came up behind them. "You

can't say you're not there. If you've said it, you are!"

"It's only me–e–e!" The sound came eerily out of the cave.

Auntie Isabel smiled. "I think I know who it is," she said. "Go inside and see."

Danny bent low and Lally followed. Danny turned on the torch, and they went deeper and deeper into the darkness of the cave. The torch beam stretched out in front of them, like Hugo Byng's last night.

Then, about ten metres ahead, they saw another long beam coming to meet theirs. Danny stepped backwards and trod on Lally's toe. "Ouch!" she squeaked. "Who's there?"

"Danny! Lally! Hello!" The voice sounded cheerful and friendly.

Danny waved the torch about, and they saw a half-bent-over figure with long blonde hair. It was Celia.

"No dinosaurs!" she said. "Only me!"

Lally giggled with relief. "I've got my

plastic dinosaurs," she said.

"Haven't you found anything?" Danny asked Celia.

"Nothing," said Celia, "except the initial discovery."

"You found a dinosaur's initials?" asked Lally.

"I do apologize. I mean, the first discovery. Last week we found… Are you cold, Lally?"

Lally was shivering. "Perishing! I want to go back out."

"No, Lally! What did you find?" asked Danny.

"Come outside, and I'll tell you."

Blinking like the squirrels in the bright sunlight, the children emerged from the cave. Celia stood up to her full height, and Danny faced her. "Please, tell us! I can't wait!"

"Last week," said Celia, "we found a very small piece of broken stone, just along the river. It gave us a hint that there might be more. The stone had a scratch on it that looked like a tiny portion of dinosaur footprint."

Lally and Danny caught their breath. "We? You and...?"

"Hugo Byng," replied Celia, as if she hated even saying the name.

"Yes," said Lally, "but who actually found it? I mean, who picked it up?"

"I did," said Celia. "But Mr Byng took it from me and said that should we find corroborative evidence – I mean, if we found any more dinosaur fossils – then he, and he alone, would decide what to do next."

"You see!" cried Lally to Danny. "He does! He only wants it for himself!"

"Sssssh," said Danny.

"That," Celia went on, "is why I decided, that day, not to work with him any longer. He is unable to co-operate reasonably on a scientific project."

"If *you* found this new evidence, what would you do with it, Celia?" asked Danny.

Lally nudged him for calling her "Celia", and he nudged her back.

"I would behave as any reputable scientist should and publish my findings immediately, so that others could take part in the great search."

Danny rounded on Lally. "You see! She's different! We can, Lally – we can let her into our secret!"

"I'm not showing her my stone!" declared Lally.

"Well, I'm showing her mine." Danny felt in his pocket.

Lally held her breath. She didn't dare scream, because it would make such an ear-splitting noise in the gorge.

"What is it, Danny?" asked Celia.

"Look," said Danny. He held out the fossil on the palm of his hand and ran his finger over the "V".

There was silence. They looked up at Celia.

Her face seemed to glow. There was no other word for it – she glowed.

"Corroborative evidence," she breathed.

"Let's get away from this horrible cave,"

said Lally. She loved the cave. But she felt torn: should she show Celia her stone too?

They walked over to where Auntie Isabel was sitting on a rock.

"Danny has shown me the most amazing find," Celia told her.

"Well!" said Auntie Isabel irritably to the children. "Your secret!"

"Only Danny!" said Lally. "I didn't show her mine!"

"But you wouldn't let me tell you Celia's secret," said Auntie Isabel.

"You didn't tell them?" said Celia. "Well, I'll tell them myself."

"I'll leave you to it," said Auntie Isabel, sounding embarrassed now. "I'll have a look inside your cave." She stood up, took the torch from Danny and walked away.

Celia took off her helmet and sat on Auntie Isabel's rock beside the river. Danny and Lally took theirs off and sat down too.

"What is your secret?" asked Danny. "We

really want to know."

Lally said nothing. But she was listening hard.

"Your aunt told me that you're adopted," said Celia. "The fact is, I'm adopted, too."

They were quite taken aback. They were certain it was something about dinosaurs.

"You can't be adopted!" said Lally. "You're grown up!"

"You mean, you're not proper, like we're not proper?" said Danny.

"Proper!" repeated Celia. "I don't understand what you mean by that. I was born like everyone else, and then I was adopted, like you were."

"Well," said Danny, wanting to get back to the subject of dinosaurs, "now Celia's told us her secret, you can show her yours, can't you, Lally?"

"I was going to," said Lally crossly. "Here." She held out her fossil. "Look – this mark, here, seems the same sort of mark as on Danny's."

Celia breathed in sharply. "Thank you –

both of you. But Lally – Danny – the vital question is this: just where did you find your stones?"

"Tell her, Lally," said Danny.

Lally opened her mouth to say, "In the stream, just up there." She glanced up, ready to point and show Celia the stream. But, before she could say a word, she shut her mouth again tight.

Peering down at them from the other side of the gorge, still wearing plastic gloves, and still dangling his hammer, was the square shape of Mr Hugo Byng.

"Not one word more." Celia spoke under her breath. "They should be placed in a sample bag... No. Hugo would see. In your pockets again – quickly."

At that moment, Auntie Isabel emerged from the cave and called to them.

"My goodness, it's chilly in there! Oh! Are you showing Celia your find?" Her voice rang out in the echoing chasm. "Is it something exciting, then? The solution to the mystery of the dinosaurs?"

High above them, there sounded a sharp plop. Mr Byng had dropped his hammer into the stream.

That evening Danny and Lally were helping to wash up Auntie Isabel's cooking pots when the phone rang.

Auntie Isabel went to the living room to answer it. Danny listened to what she was saying.

"Sssssh, Lally! I think it's them!"

"Celia and Byng-Byng?"

"No – Mum and Dad! Listen!"

"Oh, the darling!" Auntie Isabel was saying. "What about the chin – has she got Harry's chin? The poppet! Look, love, you're to take care..."

Danny said, "It's Mum!" and rushed to the phone.

"You may be up and about," Auntie Isabel went on, "but that's no reason to... Oh, here's Danny! Can he have a word? Lally, do you want a word too?"

But Lally hung back.

Danny pressed the receiver to his ear. "Mum?"

"Danny! How's it going?" The familiar voice came warmly over the phone. "Lots of playing in the river? Have you had any adventures?"

"Fine, thank you." He didn't know what to say. Oh – he ought to ask – "How's the baby?"

"Pink, a bit ugly, you know what newborn babies are like. I do miss the two of you. Is Lally OK?"

"Do you want to speak to her? Lally..."

Lally said sulkily, "Don't like telephones."

"She's fine," Danny said to his mum. "We've found some exciting stones... Bye ... here's Auntie Isabel..." Before he let the receiver go, he heard his mum say, "You're my specials." It was what their mum and dad always said to them before they went to sleep.

He stalked over to Lally. "What's wrong with you?" he hissed. "They're missing us!

She said 'You're my specials'!"

"Huh!" Lally snorted. "Special rubbish."

Auntie Isabel said goodbye and put down the phone. "Well, isn't that simply marvellous! She'll be coming out of hospital soon. Doesn't she sound exactly the same? Of course, she is exactly the same... Now. She says I'm to give you a treat. How about we try the new children's menus at the Rigby Arms? Beefburger and chips for two?"

Chapter 5

Jaysee Bee

"It's all a question of how deep they find the fossils," Danny explained to Auntie Isabel over their chips in the Rigby Arms. "If they find them this deep, where the layers are so old, it means one thing. If they find them that deep, where the layers are even older, it means something different."

"What does it mean?" Lally demanded.

"It means – oh, there's Mr Brownlow!"

The policeman and his wife had just come in. "How are my Young Detectives?" asked Mr Brownlow, walking over to their table.

"Well," said Auntie Isabel to Mrs Brownlow, glancing meaningfully at Lally, "you'll be glad to know that my sister has had a baby girl, and the two of them are doing fine."

"That's grand," beamed Mrs Brownlow.

"What will they be calling her?"

"Isabella," said Auntie Isabel. "After me."

Lally was horrified. "Isabella! People'll call her Belly-Belly!"

"Now, Laura, that's no way to speak of your new sister," said Mr Brownlow. Lally muttered under her breath, "I'm not Laura, I'm Lally."

"Have you seen Mr Byng?" asked Mr Brownlow. "The palaeontology man?"

"Er – no," said Danny. "Of course, if we do see him, we might..."

Lally kicked Danny under the table. Danny kicked her back, meaning, "I don't really mean it." But Lally kicked him again, and he looked where she was looking – towards the door.

Mr Byng, minus his plastic gloves and hammer, was walking towards them.

"Why, here's the man himself!" said Mr Brownlow. "Mr Byng! Come right here and join us!"

Mr Byng's footsteps were heavy and slow, as if his feet were as square as the rest of him. Danny and Lally held their breath. Mr

Brownlow would make them hand over their stones!

But Mr Byng didn't seem to hear Mr Brownlow. He totally ignored their table. He passed them by, with his eyes averted, and chose a table right over in the far corner, where he sat down all by himself.

"Well!" said Mr Brownlow.

"Why did he do that?" asked Danny.

"Perhaps he's shy," suggested Mrs Brownlow.

Mr Brownlow puffed on his pipe. "Mind on higher things. That'll be it. He's a man with his mind on higher things."

"I'm not sure about all this digging," said Auntie Isabel. "If they come and dig up Rugglesmoor, what will happen to our lovely hillside? Imagine Devil's Drop, if they came and dug it up to find the secret of the dinosaurs' death!"

Danny listened to them arguing about whether the progress of science came first or the beauty of the environment. He munched on his chips and watched the people of Rugglesmoor coming and going. Out stalked a gang of eighteen-year-olds, as if they longed for the Rigby Arms to transform itself into a disco. In rolled a big fat man in navy overalls and an orange plastic jacket, the sort who'd driven the gravel lorries up from Leeds.

Lally's mind started to wander. She imagined the prizes you got for making a great scientific discovery. There'd be TV interviews – reporters queuing up at your door. Would they queue up at Byng-Byng's door? Would he become Professor Hugo Byng, Big Boss of all the Pally-what-nots? But he wasn't a responsible scientist. Celia said he wasn't.

Then, suddenly, she heard Byng-Byng's voice. She remembered his voice from when he'd ordered his lightly-buttered cheese roll. It was little and rasping, like a dentist's drill.

It was saying something like, "Jaysee Bee".

She looked across the room. There was Byng-Byng, deep in conversation with the fat man in the orange jacket. He said it again:

"Mutter-mutter ... Jaysee Bee."

"Lally – Danny." Auntie Isabel had stood up and was pulling on her coat. "I've got sixty-five mushroom patties to bake and a carrot cake as well. That nice Celia's coming to tea tomorrow."

"Wait on a while," urged Mr Brownlow. "I'll go and tap our Mr Byng on the shoulder. Get him to take a peek at those stones of yours."

"No!" cried Lally.

"Er..." said Danny. "No, we're very tired and –" feeling in his pocket for his stone – "we haven't got them with us at the moment." Now it was him telling lies! Well, he had to do it to keep their precious fossils out of danger.

Auntie Isabel was amazed. "I thought you carried everything in your pockets wherever you went? Come on, it's time you two were in bed."

The next day it rained and it rained. Auntie Isabel sat Lally and Danny down in front of the fire to watch *Robin Hood* on video while she rattled away in the kitchen.

Danny was nearly asleep in his chair when he heard Lally say thoughtfully, "Jaysee Bee. What's that, Danny?"

"Dunno," said Danny, not really thinking. "Could be initials. J.C.B."

"His brother." Lally started inventing. "Joseph Christopher Byng. Jonathan Clive Byng."

"Maybe his brother'll come and help in the search." Danny could picture a brother of Hugo Byng – square, but twice as tall and very fierce. "Maybe we should tell Celia. You do trust her now, don't you?"

"I'd give her my fossil," Lally said thoughtfully. "But I don't believe her."

"What about?"

"Being adopted."

"Why not?"

"It's children who are adopted. Like us."

"She used to be our age once. Everyone used to be. Even Miss Dora."

Lally paused, then asked suddenly, "Danny, d'you remember me, when I was a baby? Before Mum and Dad got us, I mean?"

Danny turned his face away. "Sort of. I remember being in a car, and this bundle beside me, crying."

"Danny! You never said! Next thing, you'll say you remember our first mum!"

"Well, I do. Sort of. It's a kind of … blur. It's crying, too."

Lally snatched two cushions and put one against each ear. "Don't believe you! Don't want to hear!"

They watched the whole of the part about the Sheriff of Nottingham without saying a word. Then Lally said, in a little voice, "Why should they want us, Mum and Dad, now they've got a proper baby?"

"They're used to us, I suppose," said Danny. "We are special. Aren't we?"

"Don't know," said Lally, huddling further down in her chair.

* * *

By the time Celia came for tea, they'd watched three more videos and played every game in the drawer.

Celia took off her long dripping mac in the porch and swept in. "Danny – Lally! What am I going to do?"

"What's wrong?" asked Danny.

"Mr Hugo Byng," replied Celia.

"Tea and carrot cake," said Auntie Isabel, and disappeared into the kitchen.

"Does he know you've found a dinosaur footprint or does he not?" Celia flung herself into the nearest chair. "Is he going to thwart us or is he just going to work away on his own? If only he'd speak to me!"

"He's not speaking to us either," said Lally. And they told him how Byng-Byng had ignored them in the Rigby Arms.

Danny asked, "If he suspects we've got the fossils, why isn't he trying to get a look at them?"

"I know Hugo," said Celia. "He'd hate to think you've found something that he missed.

If he did look at your fossils, he'd probably accuse you of making those scratches yourselves."

Danny was outraged. "We didn't!"

"Of course you didn't. Might I just have another look? And might you, now, in the privacy of this room, tell me where you found them?"

But Lally interrupted. "Did your mum and dad ever get a proper baby?" Danny tried to stop her, but it was no good. "You got adopted same as us, but now they've got a proper baby and..."

"Well, no," said Celia. "I was an only child. I wish I'd had a brother or sister, Lally. You two have always been together, haven't you?"

Danny nodded. "We had the same first mum. She couldn't look after us."

"I didn't have anyone. I was lonely. I suppose that's why I love lonely places, like the Rugglesmoor hills."

"About brothers," put in Lally suddenly, "has Byng-Byng got one?"

"A brother? I don't think so. Why?"

"Oh, nothing. He was yakking on to a man last night, saying something like 'J.C.B.'."

"We thought he might have a big fierce brother," said Danny, "who'd come and help him dig for—"

"J.C.B!" Celia sat up straight. "Oh, no!"

Danny heard the way she said it and suddenly he knew, too. "JCB! It's a digger! Celia, do you think he's going to dig up all our hills?"

Celia's long thin face took on a long thin frown. "The man is obsessed – fanatical."

"Surely it'd break up any dinosaur footprints?"

"It would. But there is method in his madness." She spoke gravely and slowly. "As you know, the most probable place to find fossils is in sedimentary rocks, like we have here at the Gorge. That is where dinosaurs might have walked and left their footprints."

Lally's eyes widened. "You mean," she said in a hushed voice, "dinosaurs really might have walked – there – up at Devil's Drop? Right beside the stream where we found our fossils?"

"So that was where you found them. Thank you, Lally." Celia smiled. "Now, about Hugo and his digger. Sometimes the soil and rock that covers up the fossils – we call it the 'over-burden' – must be removed. With a pick or a shovel—"

"But not with a great big digger!" cried Danny.

"No, indeed." Celia took their hands. "We must stop him at all costs. We must try to find more evidence of our own and we must prevent him from gouging out Rugglesmoor with his digger. Will you help me to look wherever there might be more clues and watch out every moment for Hugo?"

Chapter 6

Mr Byng Buys Some Toys

Now they had a mission. Every day Danny and Lally climbed into Celia's old green Citroën and went up on the moor or down the Gorge. Celia gave them some plastic sheeting to kneel on. She used a geological hammer, like Mr Byng's, and gave them each a trowel. Together they examined every likely-looking stone to see if it was a fossil.

But not a fossil did they find. Celia grew quite depressed. "Nothing!" she'd exclaim, sitting back on her haunches. "Nix! Zilch! I think I'll leave it to the Germans."

"Why the Germans?" enquired Danny.

"They've found some fossilized bones in a German quarry. That's probably where the solution to the mystery lies."

Every day they looked out for signs of Hugo Byng, or his sleek Alfa Romeo, or a huge great bulldozer. They saw lambs leaping about on the grass, and the farmer on his tractor ploughing the field behind the Crown Inn. But Mr Byng was nowhere to be seen. He had vanished like the dinosaurs off the face of the earth.

Every night the children perched on the window seat, peeping through the curtains. Nothing. One night Danny woke up to hear scraping outside their bedroom window. But it was only the cat from the Rigby Arms, out on a midnight prowl.

On the fourth day, Lally said to Celia, "He's given up. He's gone home."

Danny suggested, "Maybe he's gone to Germany."

"He wouldn't do that," replied Celia. "In Germany he wouldn't be the first to make the great discovery. Hugo must always be first. Any more news of the baby?"

"Belly-Belly," said Lally in disgust.

"She's not Belly-Belly," protested Danny, "she's Isabella! She's doing fine."

"When are you going back home?"

"Don't know," said Danny. "Depends how they get on."

"I want to solve the mystery before we go," said Lally.

Celia stood up and stretched her height towards the sky. "My feelings exactly." She looked up at the heather-covered hillside, over towards the Gorge, and down to the village and the reservoir. "J – C – B. Now, where might he dig?"

"Where do you think?" asked the children.

"Anywhere," said Celia. "It could be anywhere."

Around tea time they packed up their tools and headed down the hill in Celia's car.

Outside the Post Office was parked a silver Alfa Romeo.

"Hugo!" said Celia.

"Byng-Byng!" said Lally and Danny. "Let's go and see Miss Dora. She'll know what he's up to."

Celia said, "I'll buy you some chocolate,

because you've worked so hard."

The Post Office doorbell clanged behind them. Miss Dora was standing at the counter, gazing at the door as though some apparition had just passed through it.

"Have you seen Mr Byng, Miss Dora?" Danny asked.

"It's not that we want him," said Lally. "But his car's out there and we wonder..."

"Miss Dora?" said Celia. "Is anything wrong?"

Miss Dora's voice came out faint and puzzled. "Mr Hugo Byng," she murmured. "Now what in Heaven's name...?"

"Byng-Byng? What's he been doing? Have you seen him?"

"Just now. You've missed him by no more than a minute. He came in here, leaned over the counter just like this, and asked me for a sharp penknife. Well, I've got plenty of those, for the likes of you, Danny. But then..."

"Then?"

"He said, 'And chewing-gum – with the

plastic dinosaurs.' 'I'm sorry,' I said, 'but I gave the last ones to young Lally.' Then who should come in but our lad, with a new delivery, and they've got two dinosaurs now – two to every packet!"

"Two!" exclaimed Lally. "Can I have some?"

"I asked Mr Byng what he wanted them for," said Miss Dora, "but he wouldn't let slip another word."

"Did you sell him the chewing-gum?" asked Danny.

"Fifteen packets."

"Fifteen!" Lally tried to imagine them bulging in her pocket.

"I'd no option, had I? He paid for them with a twenty-pound note!" She turned to a box behind her and took out a packet. "Here, have one for yourself, for free. He'd never have bought that amount if it hadn't been for you. Now, what was it you wanted – chocolate?"

The three of them came out of the Post

Office, and there was Mr Byng. He was leaning on the shiny bonnet of the silver Alfa Romeo, playing with plastic dinosaurs.

He raised his head and, ignoring Celia, gave Lally and Danny a forced smile.

Celia coughed. "Good afternoon, Hugo."

Mr Byng didn't reply, so she walked round the expensive Alfa Romeo to her own ancient car. The children hesitated, intrigued by the sight of a palaeontologist playing with plastic dinosaurs.

"No! How simply maddening!" Celia's cry had them running round to the Citroën.

"It's your tyre," said Danny. "It's gone squidgy."

"It must be a slow puncture," said Celia. "I'd better take it down to the garage before it gets any worse. But what about you two?"

"We can walk," said Lally. "See you tomorrow."

"Good luck with the tyre!" called Danny, as Celia climbed in and drove off slowly down the hill. Lally was gazing at the menagerie of extinct beasts that sat on the silver bonnet.

"I believe," said Mr Byng in his small, rasping voice, "that you young people take an interest in palaeontology."

"Dinosaurs," said Lally.

"But these are not all dinosaurs." He spoke very precisely, as though he were spitting. "This, for instance, with paddle-like limbs, is a plesiosaur. One must be exact, mustn't one? One must never make a mistake about facts. And this –" he pushed forward one with wings – "is a pterosaur, from the Jurassic or Cretaceous Period." Such a long speech from Mr Byng made the children's mouths hang open. "I have more of these items." His freckled hands delved into the many pockets of his brown tweed jacket, and Danny and Lally gawped as he took out one plastic dinosaur after another and laid them down, side by side.

"That's what you want, isn't it?" he said, his voice more than ever like a dentist's drill.

"Little dinosaurs. Plastic stegosauruses. Toy pterodactyls. Not proper palaeontology. Now, you play with those," he went on, "like good children, and –" he turned on them with eyes like swords – "you leave my hillsides alone!"

He took a polythene bag out of his top pocket, swept the dinosaurs into it, thrust the bag into Danny's hand and turned on his heel. Then he trotted through the garden gate to his cottage.

"Well!" said Danny.

"He's mad!" said Lally.

But mad or not, he'd given them the dinosaurs. "I'll have a whole village of them," said Lally excitedly, as they set off down the hill towards home.

"We've got a real dinosaur now," said Danny. "You don't need plastic ones."

Lally stopped for a moment, and thought. "I had the plastic ones first," she said finally. "They're special." They strode on.

The farmer had finished ploughing the field

behind the Crown Inn and was unhitching the plough from his tractor. Lally and Danny recognized him – he was red-haired Nick, the son of the people who kept the Rigby Arms. He called to them, “Danny, Laura! Brisk day, then?”

“It’s not Laura, it’s Lally!” called Lally. But Nick was too busy to hear. He was picking up some fence posts to put in the back of his small open-backed truck.

Past the Crown Inn they could see down to the next bend. It was a sharp bend with the usual grey stone wall winding alongside.

Crashed against the stone wall was the old green Citroën.

“Celia!” shouted Danny and Lally. They ran.

Chapter 7

Confrontation

“There’s no one in it!” cried Lally as they got near. But at the sound of their voices a head with long blonde hair rose up from behind the car.

“He did it!” said Celia. “Oh, my poor car!”

“Byng-Byng? Did what?”

“The tyre collapsed as soon as I drove off. That was no slow puncture – that was a double-quick one.”

Lally and Danny went round and looked at the damage to the car. Its wing was dented right in, the green metal crumpled like a piece of old rag.

“But how could Byng-Byng do it?” asked Danny. “He’s only got a hammer and a trowel!”

“Do you remember what Miss Dora said?” asked Celia grimly. “Hugo asked for chewing-gum and a—"

"Penknife!" cried Lally.

"Exactly," said Celia.

She pointed. Now the tyre was down, they could see a neat, purposeful-looking slit.

Lally said, "He must have done it, while—"

"While we were talking to Miss Dora," said Danny. "To stop you looking for fossils!"

"And he bought us those dinosaurs," said Lally, "so that—"

"So we'd be too busy to look for real ones!" finished Danny.

Lally gave him a push. "Don't keep on saying what I wanted to say!"

"You're right," said Celia. "Hugo wants us out of his way. And why?"

"So he can—" started Danny.

"Dig up the hillside with his Jaysee Bee!" finished Lally triumphantly. "Celia! What are we going to do?"

"I'm afraid that my first task must be to alert the police," said Celia. "I could have been killed by his ruthless action on my tyre.

Fossils and dinosaurs must take second place to that."

They looked at her and realized what a shock she'd just had. Her face was white and her fingers were knotted tightly together.

"Shall we come with you to Mr Brownlow's?" asked Danny.

"No, I'll be all right." She unknotted her fingers and gave herself a little shake. "Might you go back to the Post Office? You could tell Miss Dora what happened and keep a watch on Hugo's movements from there."

"We'll do that," said Danny.

The two of them watched the lanky figure making her way shakily down the hill in the grey light of late afternoon. Then they linked hands and ran back up towards the square.

"Hey!" shouted Nick the farmer, coming through the gate. "What's the rush?" But they couldn't explain.

The fountain still trickled water that would make you healthy, wealthy and stout. But where Mr Hugo Byng's sleek sports car had stood, with dinosaurs on its bonnet, was an empty space.

"He's gone!" cried Lally.

They ran into the Post Office.

Miss Dora was just locking up the till. "Too late," she said. "No crisps or chewing-gum. I'm shutting up shop."

"It's not that," puffed Danny. "Did you see Byng-Byng?"

"See him I did not," said Miss Dora. "Hear him I did, in that ridiculous machine of his. Should be on a motor-road, that sort of vehicle, not up here among the peace and quiet."

"Motorway," corrected Lally. "Which way did he go?"

"Up that there hill, and a deal too fast!"

"He tried to get us out of the way –" said Danny.

"So he can dig up the hillside," finished Lally, "without any of us seeing!"

"Dig up the hillside?" repeated Miss Dora. "He can't do that – not without getting permission off the Parish Council. And that means me!"

"But, Miss Dora," said Lally, "you know that penknife that Byng-Byng wanted? Well, he went and cut Celia's tyre with it!"

"Mercy's sake! To do a thing like—" Miss Dora stopped as the doorbell rattled and clanged. The children whirled round. Mr Byng?

No, it was Nick the farmer. "Not shut, are you, Miss Dora? The wife asked me to get some sugar on my way home."

Danny and Lally turned to each other, the same thought in their head.

"Have you got your tractor?" Danny asked Nick.

"To drive up the hill?" added Lally.

"I'm in the truck now," said Nick. "Why up the hill?"

"Please can we jump in the back –"

"To get up the hill –"

"To find the JCB –"

"And stop Mr Byng!"

"That's what's got to be done," said Miss Dora. "You wanted sugar, young Nick?" She shoved a packet of sugar into Nick's hand. "Pay me next week, or whenever you like. The truck's outside, is it?"

"Could somebody tell me just what's going on?" asked red-haired Nick.

So Danny and Lally and Miss Dora told him.

"If I shift these fence posts, you two kids can just about squeeze in," said Nick, outside. "Only, hang on tight! See you later, Miss Dora."

"Think I'm staying behind?" said Miss Dora. "I'm a Parish Councillor! Look here, young Nick. I used to push you round in your pram. Who drove the tractor when there was muck-spreading to be done and all of Rugglesmoor down with the flu? Your Miss Dora! So it's me that's driving up this hill in this truck!"

Nick's round red face fell like a little boy's. "She's a grand tractor driver," he told the children. "Brought up on a farm. All right, Miss Dora. Into the driving seat with you. But I'll get back to the farm for my motorbike and I'll be up there before you can say Jack Robinson."

Lally and Danny could hardly believe it. Nick shifted the fence posts and they clambered in. Miss Dora climbed into the driving seat and started up the engine as if she did it every day of the week. Then they were off.

They were probably only driving at twenty miles an hour, but the cold wind blew in their faces as if they were going at seventy. The sky was gloomy and grey. Miss Dora even tried to put on the truck's headlights, but she was concentrating so hard on the road, she couldn't find the knob that worked them.

Danny whispered into Lally's ear, "And I haven't thought about our baby all day!"

"Nor have I," Lally whispered back. "Danny – are we really proper? Will Mum and Dad ever come for us?"

They rounded sharp bends, went grinding in low gear up the long hill – and as they neared the top, Danny realized that this wasn't just an adventure. This was danger. Byng-Byng was so desperate to get fossils of his very own that he'd risked Celia's life. He might risk theirs too. And they were eight and ten, and Miss Dora, brilliant truck driver or no, was a hundred and five – well, seventy-one.

Round another bend and they'd be at the top of the hill.

"What about that man in the Rigby Arms?" Danny said into Lally's ear. "The JCB one. What was he like?"

"Big and fat," said Lally. "A tyranno-saurus."

Miss Dora looked over her shoulder and pointed ahead.

"There they are!" shouted Lally.

Hugo Byng's silver sports car was parked in a space where tourists stopped to admire the view. Beside it, blocking the road, stood a huge yellow digger. Its wheels were gigantic.

At the back they could see an enormous scoop, and at the front was its massive front-loader that could shift tons of soil and rock in minutes.

High up in the driving seat, behind the windscreen of the cab, was the fat man Lally had seen in the Rigby Arms. Squeezed in beside him sat Mr Byng.

As soon as he saw them, Mr Byng waved his fist. The fat man shouted, "Get out of the way!"

"No!" Miss Dora shouted back.

"You are blocking the road!" shouted Mr Byng through the windscreen.

"So are you!" shouted Miss Dora.

Lally clutched Danny. Danny knocked on the window to Miss Dora. "They're bigger than we are!"

Miss Dora ignored him and got out of the truck. Standing and facing the JCB, she called, "I am a member of Rugglesmoor Parish Council! You have no official permission to dig!"

"Come on," decided Danny. "We've got to stick up for her!" Lally nodded, her heart pounding, and they both climbed down onto the road.

Miss Dora shouted, "I forbid you to move that vehicle one inch forward!" The fat man's answer was to switch his headlights full on, to dazzle their eyes.

Mr Byng leaned over. "Desist from these senseless gestures!" he hissed. Then the digger's engine switched on, and its massive front-loader lifted and groaned. The engine roared. The JCB started to move.

"They'll run us down!" screamed Lally.

"Back to the truck!" ordered Miss Dora. She climbed into the driving seat, and the children grazed their knees as they scrambled into the back. Miss Dora started up the engine – but they didn't move.

"Miss Dora!" cried Danny. "Reverse!"

"I'm trying…" began Miss Dora, pushing and pulling at the gear stick. "I don't know how this gets into reverse gear!"

Lally couldn't bear to look. She covered up her eyes to stop her seeing the digger's great front-loader, with the giant-sized wheels behind. It would crush the little truck to pieces, it would scrunch all three of them in one mouthful... One grinding, crushing scrunch, and they'd be mangled and crumpled like paper, like the wing of Celia's poor car...

But with her eyes covered, her ears could hear better. Mixed with the roar of the JCB were other noises, coming from behind. "Danny!" she called, keeping her fingers tight over her eyes. "What's that? It's a siren!"

"The police!" cried Danny. "And Nick –"

The digger's engine still roared, but its wheels crunched more slowly, then stopped. Nick's motorbike, with a roar, overtook the truck and braked, with a screech, between them and the JCB.

"And there's Auntie Isabel," Danny went on breathlessly, "and another car, a bit like ours... Lally, look!"

Chapter 8

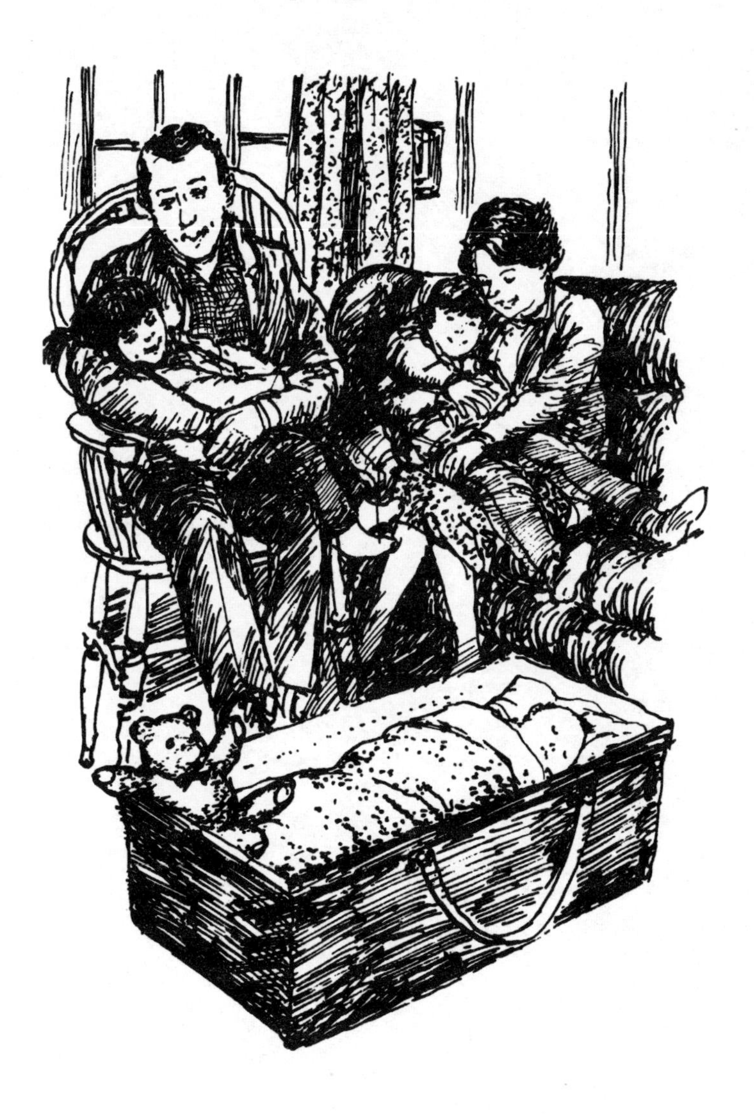

Goodbye, Dinosaur

Lally took her hands away from her eyes. Together, squashed in the back of the truck, the two of them blinked at the sight of it all.

Miss Dora jumped down from the driving seat and started to harangue Mr Byng. Nick hauled the fat JCB driver down from the cab and started shouting at him as if he'd known him all his life, which he probably had. Celia and Auntie Isabel tried to explain to Mr Brownlow why Mr Byng had got hold of the digger in the first place.

Mr Brownlow was saying to Mr Byng and the JCB driver, "I think you've got a bit of explaining to do", while leading them to the police car. Miss Dora was telling Nick that she wanted to drive the truck back down the hill, even though, at that moment, she looked at least a hundred and five years old.

It was a moment of total confusion. In the middle of it all, while Nick was helping them down from the back of the truck, the children heard voices calling, "Danny! Lally!" They sounded familiar, like... But they couldn't be. Mum and Dad were busy with the new baby, back home.

Then they looked at the other car, the one that Danny had described as "a bit like ours". It'd had to park some way away, so that it didn't block the road. Now that the children could see the car, they realized it wasn't just a bit like theirs. It was theirs.

Mum and Dad had got out and were walking towards them. They were smiling. They hadn't changed! They looked exactly the same as they'd always done.

"Mum! Dad!" cried Danny, and rushed into two huge hugs. Lally hung back.

"I couldn't think what was happening," Auntie Isabel was saying, with Celia standing beside her. "First Celia came running with her story of Mr Byng stabbing her tyre – then

Mr Brownlow said he must rush up and stop him digging up the hillside – I was just getting into the car when there was a 'peep-peep' of a horn, and who should be there standing but..."

"Lally?" said Mum. Dad let go of Danny and held out his arms.

"We *are* your specials!" cried Lally, and ran.

"Let's go home," said Auntie Isabel.

"Let's," said Lally.

They'd already peered inside their car to see the carry-cot in the back. A little bundle of blankets stirred and went on sleeping.

But Danny said, "No – wait. Lally. What are we going to do with our dinosaur fossils?"

"What?" Mum and Dad looked amazed. "Actual fossils, of dinosaurs, here?"

"Footprints!" said Lally. "And we found them!"

"So that was your secret!" exclaimed Auntie Isabel.

Celia came forward and spoke to their parents. "Let me explain. Hugo Byng and I were investigating, here in Rugglesmoor, the mystery of the dinosaurs' extinction. Imagine my delight when we found a small piece of evidence – and then had it confirmed by Danny and Lally's find."

The children fumbled among the rubbish at the bottom of their pockets and took out their precious stones. In the gloom, Mum and Dad and Auntie Isabel peered for the first time at the curious marks.

"Of course," Celia went on, "the most important finds have been made in other parts of the world—"

Mum interrupted. "But Danny, Lally, why didn't you hand the fossils straight over to Ms Marchbanks and Mr Byng?"

"We didn't trust them," said Lally. "We thought they were just out for themselves."

"I'm sorry, Celia," said Danny.

"I understand," Celia replied. "You were sensible not to trust Hugo."

"But you're all right," said Lally.

"Well," said Celia, "we've got something in common, haven't we?"

"In common?" asked Dad. "What?"

"Tell you later," said Lally. "Danny, what'll we do with our fossils?"

"Celia," said Danny, "if we gave them to you, what would you do with them?"

"I should give them to the appropriate scientific institution, so that further investigations could be made in the correct manner."

Danny and Lally looked at each other.

"OK?" asked Danny.

"OK," agreed Lally.

And, with a great sigh, they slid their stones into Celia's long, bony, responsible hand.

When Celia had gone and the rest of them were safely back in the house, Auntie Isabel bustled into the kitchen saying, "Really, a good hot drink is what we all need."

Danny sat with Mum's arm round him on the sofa, and Lally sat with Dad's arm round her in the big chair. Baby Bella, who hadn't made a sound during all the goings-on, lay fast asleep in the corner.

"You knew!" said Lally. "You knew something was happening, and you came!"

"We didn't know a thing," said Dad.

"I just said, 'I can't be without them a minute longer'," said Mum. "And your dad said, 'Neither can I'. So we got in the car and drove."

"And when we got here," said Dad, "and Isabel said you were saving Rugglesmoor from a mad archaeologist, what could we do but follow them up there?"

"He's not an archaeologist, he's a palaeontologist," said Danny.

"Show-off," said Lally.

Auntie Isabel had made some gooey chocolate buns. Danny ate four and Lally ate five. They were both, suddenly, completely exhausted.

"Mum, Dad," said Lally sleepily, "people keep on calling me Laura. But I make them call me Lally. Why did you call our baby Bella? They'll call her Belly-Belly at school."

"Not if we don't let them," said Danny.

"We won't always be there!"

"We've got to look after her!"

"Stop bossing me about," said Lally. She closed her eyes.

There was silence for a minute.

"She's gone to sleep," Danny whispered to Mum.

"Haven't, so there," said Lally, without opening her eyes.

"Arguing as usual," grinned Dad. "Some things never change."